# JOHN A·ROWE **BABY CROW**

**A MICHAEL NEUGEBAUER BOOK**

COPYRIGHT © 1994 BY MICHAEL NEUGEBAUER VERLAG AG
FIRST PUBLISHED IN SWITZERLAND UNDER THE TITLE RABEN-BABY
BY MICHAEL NEUGEBAUER VERLAG AG, GOSSAU ZURICH.

PUBLISHED IN THE UNITED STATES, GREAT BRITAIN, AUSTRALIA, AND NEW ZEALAND IN 1994
BY NORTH-SOUTH BOOKS, AN IMPRINT OF NORD-SÜD VERLAG.

DISTRIBUTED IN THE UNITED STATES BY NORTH-SOUTH BOOKS, INC., NEW YORK.

LIBRARY OF CONGRESS CATALOGING-IN-PUBLICATION DATA IS AVAILABLE
A CIP CATALOGUE RECORD FOR THIS BOOK IS AVAILABLE FROM THE BRITISH LIBRARY
ISBN 1-55858-277-0 (TRADE EDITION)
ISBN 1-55858-278-9 (LIBRARY EDITION)

10 9 8 7 6 5 4 3 2 1
PRINTED IN BELGIUM

# BABY CROW

### JOHN A. ROWE

NORTH-SOUTH BOOKS · NEW YORK · LONDON

ONCE UPON A TIME, IN A TALL HOLLOW TREE,
THERE LIVED A FLOCK OF CROWS.
AT NIGHT THEY WOULD HANG THEIR HATS
OUTSIDE THEIR ROOMS BEFORE THEY WENT
TO SLEEP.

THE OLDEST CROWS LIVED AT THE TOP OF THE TREE. THE BRANCHES WERE THINNER UP THERE, WHICH MADE IT EASIER TO WEAR THEIR HATS. THEY SPENT MOST OF EACH DAY EITHER SLEEPING OR DISCUSSING THE PRICES OF NEW HATS.

GRANDFATHER CROW LIVED AT THE VERY TOP OF THE TREE. HE WAS OLD AND WISE. HE HAD LOST MANY OF THE FEATHERS IN HIS PLUMAGE, BUT HE STILL HAD HIS BEAUTIFUL VOICE.
IN HIS YOUTH, GRANDFATHER CROW HAD BEEN A FAMOUS OPERA SINGER. PEOPLE STILL CAME FROM FAR AWAY TO HEAR HIM SING.

OTHER TALENTED SINGERS LIVED TOWARDS THE BOTTOM OF THE TREE. THEY WOULD PROUDLY BELT OUT THEIR SONGS, AND THEY WORE THEIR AWARD MEDALS ON RIBBONS AROUND THEIR NECKS.

AND AT THE VERY BOTTOM OF THE TREE
LIVED BABY CROW. HIS FAMILY WAS PROUD
OF HIM, FOR THEY KNEW HE WAS GOING
TO BE A GREAT SINGER WHEN HE GREW UP.
BUT USUALLY BABY CROW JUST SAT IN
HIS NEST STARING OUT AT THE WORLD
AROUND HIM.

■

ONE DAY, WHEN FATHER CROW COULD WAIT NO LONGER, HE WENT TO BABY CROW AND SAID: "MY SON, IT'S TIME THAT YOU BEGAN TO SING. SAY KAAAAAW!"

"BEEP," SAID BABY CROW.

"NO...MUCH LOUDER," SAID FATHER CROW.

"BEEEEEEP," SAID BABY CROW, AS LOUDLY AS HE COULD.

FATHER CROW COULDN'T BELIEVE HIS EARS.

"MY BABY ISN'T A REAL CROW! HE CAN'T SING. WHAT SHALL I DO?" HE CRIED.

THAT MADE BABY CROW VERY SAD.
HE WANTED TO BE A REAL CROW.
SADLY HE HOPPED AWAY FROM THE TREE.
MOTHER CROW CALLED HIM BACK.
"LET ME TRY," SHE SAID. "NOW BABY CROW,
BREATHE DEEPLY, OPEN YOUR BEAK WIDE,
AND SING LIKE THIS...KAAAAAW!"
BABY CROW BREATHED IN...OPENED HIS
BEAK WIDE...AND SANG: "BEEEEEEP!"
FATHER CROW SHOOK HIS FEATHERS.
"WHAT SHOULD WE DO?" HE MOANED.
"TAKE HIM TO SEE GRANDFATHER CROW,"
SAID MOTHER CROW. "HE'LL KNOW WHAT
TO DO!"

■

"PLEASE HELP US, GRANDFATHER CROW," PLEADED FATHER CROW. "OUR BABY CAN'T SING. ALL HE CAN SAY IS BEEP!"

"HMMM..." SAID GRANDFATHER CROW AS HE SCRATCHED HIS HEAD. "LET ME THINK A MOMENT." HE TURNED TO BABY CROW. "SAY AAH."

"EEEEEP," SAID BABY CROW.

"HMMM..." SAID GRANDFATHER CROW. "THIS IS MORE SERIOUS THAN I THOUGHT. SAY DO-RE-ME."

"BEEEEEP...BEEEEEP...BEEEEEP," SAID BABY CROW.

■

GRANDFATHER CROW GENTLY OPENED BABY CROW'S BEAK WITH ONE CLAW.

"COUGH FOR ME, MY BOY."

BABY CROW DID AS HE WAS TOLD, AND WHEN HE COUGHED, A LARGE RED CHERRY THAT HAD BEEN STUCK IN HIS THROAT FOR SOME TIME SHOT OUT AND HIT GRANDFATHER CROW IN THE BEAK.

"OUCH!" SCREAMED GRANDFATHER CROW. "LET THAT BE A LESSON TO YOU! CHEW YOUR FOOD BEFORE YOU SWALLOW IT!"

"KAAAAAW!" SANG BABY CROW, SO LOUDLY THAT EVERYONE LEAPT INTO THE AIR WITH FRIGHT.

"MY SON!" CRIED FATHER CROW WITH DELIGHT. "YOU CAN SING—SO LOUDLY!"

■

"KAAAAAW! KAAAAAW! KAAAAAW!" SANG BABY CROW AGAIN. HE WAS SO PLEASED TO BE A REAL CROW THAT HE WANTED THE WHOLE WORLD TO HEAR HIM.

"KAAAAAW! KAAAAAW! KAAAAAW!" ALL THROUGH THE NIGHT, WHILE THE OTHER CROWS TRIED THEIR BEST TO SLEEP, HE SANG AND SANG AND SANG.

"MY SON," SAID FATHER CROW WEARILY, "COULD YOU PERHAPS SING A LITTLE QUIETER?"

"KAAAAAW! KAAAAAW! KAAAAAW!" SANG BABY CROW LOUDER THAN EVER.

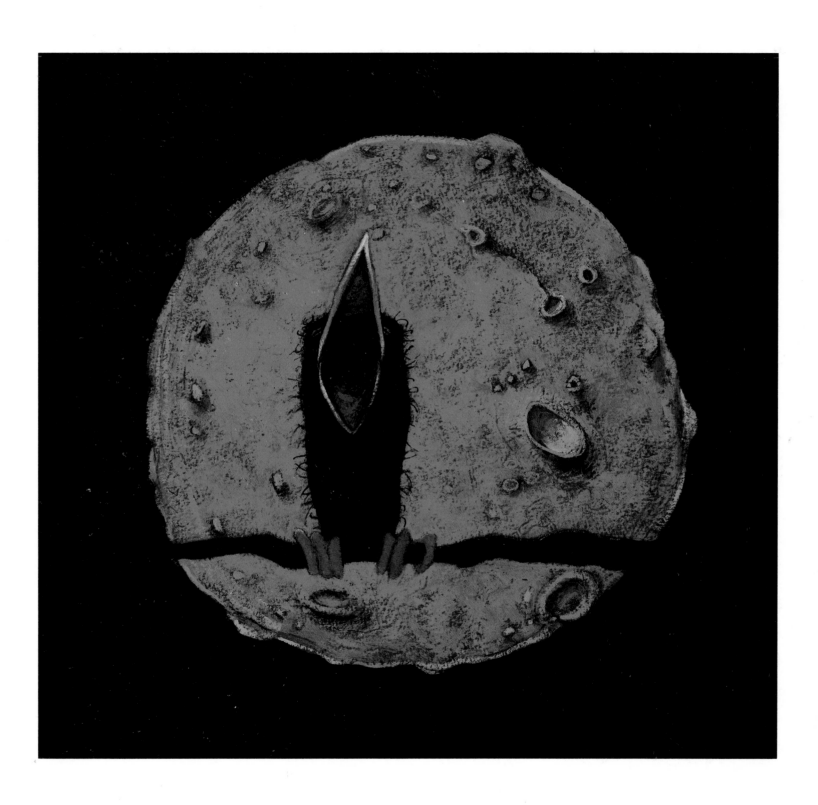

"OH DEAR," SAID MOTHER CROW, "I THINK I LIKED IT BETTER WHEN BABY CROW COULDN'T SING!"

"US TOO!" AGREED ALL THE OTHER CROWS IN THE TREE, PLUGGING THEIR EARS WITH CHERRIES.

"HE SANG 'BEEP' SO NICELY BEFORE!" SAID A TIRED CROW FROM THE NEXT TREE, WHO HADN'T SLEPT A WINK ALL NIGHT.

"I HAVE AN IDEA!" SAID FATHER CROW EXCITEDLY, AND HE FLEW OFF IN SEARCH OF THE CLOSEST CHERRY TREE.

■

"WOULD YOU LIKE A FEW CHERRIES?"
HE SAID TO THE TIRELESS SINGER WHEN HE
RETURNED.
"KAAAAAW! KAAAAAW! KAAAAAW!"
ANSWERED BABY CROW, GREEDILY
GOBBLING UP THE CHERRIES.
"WELL, HOW DO THEY TASTE?" ASKED
FATHER CROW.
BABY CROW ANSWERED: "BEEP!"
"WELL DONE!" SAID ALL THE OTHER CROWS.

■

"NOW BABY CROW CAN SING AS MUCH AS HE WANTS, AND WE'LL HAVE PEACE AND QUIET," SAID FATHER CROW.
THE FLOCK OF CROWS WAS CONVINCED THAT BABY CROW WOULD ONE DAY SING AS BEAUTIFULLY AS GRANDFATHER CROW, AND THAT PEOPLE WOULD COME FROM FAR AND WIDE TO HEAR HIM.

■